# THUMP and PLUNK

STORY BY
*Janice May Udry*

PICTURES BY
*Geoffrey Hayes*

HarperCollins*Publishers*

For information address HarperCollins
Children's Books, a division of HarperCollins Publishers,
195 Broadway, New York, NY 10007.
www.harperchildrens.com
Manufactured in China. 

Library of Congress Cataloging-in-Publication Data
Udry, Janice May.
Thump and Plunk / by Janice May Udry ; pictures by Geoffrey Hayes.
p. cm. — (A my first I can read book)
Summary: When Thump thumps Plunk's doll Plunkit, an argument starts that their mother resolves.
ISBN 0-06-028528-1. — ISBN 0-06-028529-X (lib. bdg.)
ISBN 0-06-444267-5 (pbk.)
[1. Brothers and sisters—Fiction.] I. Hayes, Geoffrey, ill. II. Title. III. Series.
PZ7.U27Ti 2000 99-10510
[E]—dc21 CIP

18 SCP 20 19 18
❖
Newly illustrated edition

Visit us on the World Wide Web!
www.harperchildrens.com

# THUMP and PLUNK

Here are Thump and Plunk,
with their dolls,
Thumpit and Plunkit.

Thump and Plunk sit still
and look at their toes.

Then Plunk plunks
Thump's Thumpit.

So Thump thumps Plunk.

And Plunk plunks Thump.

So Thump
thumps Plunk again.
And Plunk
plunks Thump again.

They plunk and thump
and thump and plunk
each other until—

“Plunk!” says their mother.

“Stop plunking Thump!”

"Thump thumped me first,"
cries Plunk.

"Thump!" says their mother.
"Did you thump
Plunk first
or did Plunk plunk
you first?"

“I thumped Plunk first,”
says Thump.
“She plunked my Thumpit!”

“Plunk,” says their mother,

“did you plunk

Thump’s Thumpit?”

“Yes I did,” says Plunk.
“I plunked Thumpit.
He is a doll.
It did not hurt him.”

“All the same,”
says their mother,
“you may plunk Plunkit
but do not plunk Thumpit.

And do not plunk Thump.

Ever."

"Yes, Mother," says Plunk.

"And Thump,"
says their mother,
"no more thumping Plunk.
Or Plunkit."
"Yes, Mother," says Thump.

"All right,"
says their mother.
"Now let's all go
for a nice swim."